The Dance Fairies

For my cousin Becky,

who could outwit the goblins every time,

Special thanks to

Narinder Dhami

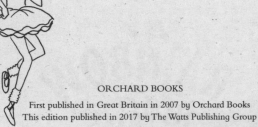

ORCHARD BOOKS

First published in Great Britain in 2007 by Orchard Books
This edition published in 2017 by The Watts Publishing Group

3 5 7 9 10 8 6 4 2

Copyright © 2017 Rainbow Magic Limited.
Copyright © 2017 HIT Entertainment Limited.
Cover illustrations © Georgie Ripper, 2007
Inside illustrations © Orchard Books, 2007

HiT entertainment

A CIP catalogue record for this book is available from the British Library.

ISBN 978 1 40830 344 3

Printed in Great Britain by Clays Ltd, Elcograf S.p.A.

MIX
Paper from
responsible sources
FSC® C104740

The paper and board used in this book are made from wood from responsible sources

Orchard Books
An imprint of Hachette Children's Group
Part of The Watts Publishing Group Limited
Carmelite House, 50 Victoria Embankment, London EC4Y 0DZ

An Hachette UK Company
www.hachette.co.uk
www.hachettechildrens.co.uk

Bethany the Ballet Fairy

by Daisy Meadows

Join the **Rainbow Magic Reading Challenge!**

Read the story and collect your fairy points to climb the Reading Rainbow at the back of the book.

This book is worth 5 points.

Hold tight to the ribbons, please.
You goblins now may feel a breeze.
I'm summoning a hurricane
To take the ribbons away again.

But, goblins, you'll be swept up too,
For I have work for you to do.
Guard each ribbon carefully,
By using this new power to freeze.

Contents

Fairies in a Whirl

"I'm *really* looking forward to this!" exclaimed Rachel Walker to her best friend, Kirsty Tate. "I *love* ballet."

"Me, too," Kirsty agreed, raising her voice above the noise of the train as it rattled over a bumpy bit of track. "I've never seen *Swan Lake* before."

"I've heard that this is a fantastic

production," Kirsty's mum said. "The
scenery is supposed to be gorgeous."

"Well, let's hope it keeps
Dad awake!" Kirsty
laughed, glancing at
her dad who was fast
asleep in the corner
seat. "I'm so pleased
you could come,
Rachel. Wasn't it
lucky that your school finished for
half-term the day before ours? You
wouldn't have been here in time to
come with us otherwise."

Rachel nodded. Because their families
lived quite a long way apart, she was
staying with Kirsty for the whole week
of the half-term holiday.

"We'll be in London soon," said

Mrs Tate, as the train drew into
a station. "This is the last stop before
we get there."

Kirsty stared out of the window as the
train slowed. Suddenly her attention was
caught by a flash of icy blue streaking
past the window. Puzzled, Kirsty leaned
forward for a closer look.

To her amazement, she saw seven
little fairies being tumbled
through the air by
a tiny icy
whirlwind.
As Kirsty
watched,
the fairies
landed safely in
one of the baskets of flowers suspended
from the station roof.

Kirsty and Rachel knew a lot about fairies because the two girls shared an amazing secret. They were best friends with the fairies, and had often helped them to defeat mean Jack Frost and his naughty goblin servants, who were always causing trouble. Now it looked as if their fairy friends might need the girls' help once more.

Almost bursting with excitement, Kirsty glanced at Rachel. But she could see that her friend hadn't noticed anything. "Mum, I'm feeling hungry," Kirsty said quickly. "Do you think Rachel and I could go and get some biscuits from the buffet car?"

Mrs Tate nodded. "But not too many," she warned. "Remember we're going out for dinner after the show."

Kirsty nodded as she and Rachel got up from their seats.

"Rachel, I've just seen *seven* fairies on the station platform!" Kirsty gasped, as soon as they'd left the carriage.

Rachel looked thrilled. "Seven fairies!" she exclaimed. "Where?"

"Right here!" Kirsty said, pulling down the window that lay directly opposite the basket of fairies. "Hello!" she called softly, hoping the fairies would hear her.

The fairies were dusting themselves off among the pansies, but at the sound of Kirsty's voice, one of them looked up and saw the girls. Her tiny face lit up, and a moment later all seven fairies were zooming over to join Kirsty and Rachel. They flew inside the train and Kirsty shut the window.

"You're Rachel and Kirsty!" declared one of the fairies, happily. "I've seen you with the King and Queen in Fairyland."

The girls smiled at the tiny fairy, who was dressed in a sparkling white tutu and pink ballet shoes. "I'm so pleased you're here," the fairy went on. "We're the Dance Fairies. I'm Bethany the Ballet Fairy, and this is Jade the Disco Fairy, Rebecca the Rock 'n' Roll Fairy, Tasha the Tap Dance Fairy, Jessica the Jazz Fairy, Saskia the Salsa Fairy and Imogen the Ice Dance Fairy."

Rachel and Kirsty smiled at the fairies, feeling quite dazzled by their gorgeous outfits. The fairies managed to smile back, but the girls could see that their eyes were sad and their sparkling wings drooped.

"Has something gone wrong?" asked Rachel.

Bethany nodded. "It's Jack Frost!" she announced miserably. "He's just cast a spell to throw us out of Fairyland and into the human world. That's why we're here. But, worst of all, he's stolen our magic Dance Ribbons!"

Jack Frost Spells Trouble

"Oh, no!" Rachel exclaimed. "Jack Frost's up to his old tricks again!"

"What exactly do the ribbons do?" asked Kirsty.

"They make sure that all dancing goes well and is fun, both in Fairyland and in the human world," Bethany explained. "But the ribbons will only

work properly if they are each attached
to the right fairy's wand. If we don't
get our ribbons back, nobody will be
able to dance properly ever again!"

Rachel and Kirsty stared at each
other in horror.

"That's terrible!" Kirsty exclaimed.

"Is there anything we can do to
help?" Rachel asked.

Bethany smiled gratefully at them.

"Thank you, girls!" she
cried. "Even though
Jack Frost's spell cast
us into the human
world, a little bit of
fairy magic must have
helped to bring us here to
you! Will you come to Fairyland with
us, so that we can tell the King and

Queen what's happened?"

"We'd love to, but what about my mum and dad?" asked Kirsty. "They'll wonder where we are."

"Fairy magic will make sure you return to the human world as if no time has passed," Bethany replied reassuringly.

Rachel and Kirsty grinned and Bethany showered the girls with white and pink glittering fairy dust. As the magical sparkles floated down around them, the girls shrank to fairy-size and translucent wings appeared on their shoulders.

Next moment, the girls were whizzing through the air in a haze of fairy dust, and, in no time at all, they were hovering above the golden Fairyland palace with its four pink turrets.

The King and Queen were strolling in the palace gardens. They looked extremely surprised to see the seven Dance Fairies, as well as Rachel and Kirsty, fluttering towards them.

"Good afternoon, Dance Fairies!"

King Oberon called. "And welcome,
Kirsty and Rachel."

"How are you, girls?" asked Queen
Titania, smiling kindly at Kirsty and
Rachel. "Do you need our help?"

"No, Your Majesty," Rachel replied,
shaking her head.

"It's us Dance Fairies who need Kirsty
and Rachel's help, Your Majesties!"
Bethany declared. "Jack Frost has just
stolen our magic Dance Ribbons!"

The King and Queen frowned.

"He sent us all hurtling into the human world too," Bethany went on. "But, luckily, fairy magic led us to Kirsty and Rachel, and then we all came back to Fairyland to tell you what had happened."

"Let's see exactly what went on," said Queen Titania, leading the way to the golden pool in the palace gardens. The Queen waved her wand over the pool and then nodded at Bethany.

The Ballet Fairy immediately touched her wand gently to the water and ripples began to spread across its surface.

"As Your Majesties already know, Jack Frost was fed up because whenever he throws a party, none of his goblins can dance properly!" Bethany explained. "So today, Jack Frost asked the other Dance Fairies and me to teach the goblins how to dance."

"We thought it meant that Jack Frost had changed his ways and wanted to be friends with us," Jade the Disco Fairy put in. "But we were wrong!"

Everyone watched as a picture appeared in the pool. Rachel and Kirsty saw the seven Dance Fairies knocking on the door of Jack Frost's ice castle.

"Are those the magic ribbons?" asked Kirsty, pointing at the fairies' wands in the picture. Each fairy had a ribbon trailing from the tip of her wand. Bethany nodded as the picture changed to show Jack Frost opening the door. His cold, sulky face broke into a smile as he saw the Dance Fairies waiting outside.

"Come in!" he cried, "We're all ready for you!"

Rachel and Kirsty watched as Jack Frost led the Dance Fairies into the throne room. There his goblin servants were lined up, dressed in their finest outfits. They wore outsized hats with large plumed feathers, embroidered

waistcoats and velvet trousers. Rachel
and Kirsty smiled. They'd never seen
the goblins look quite like this before!

Jack Frost sat down on his magnificent
ice throne, and watched as the Dance
Fairies began the lesson.

The goblins were *terrible* dancers.

They stumbled across the throne room, frequently tripping over their own feet and each other's. Then they started arguing, and their yelling drowned out the beautiful music that the Dance Fairies had conjured up.

But, as Rachel and Kirsty watched, the Dance Fairies quickly began to work their magic. Gradually the goblins stopped bumping into each other and arguing, and began gliding around the room in time to the music instead.

Kirsty nudged Rachel. "Look, even Jack Frost seems to be enjoying himself!" she pointed out.

Jack Frost was sitting on his throne, merrily tapping his foot along to the music. But, suddenly, he jumped up from his seat, a spiteful smile on his face. "NOW!" he bellowed.

Immediately the goblins dashed forward and grabbed all seven ribbons from the Dancc Fairies' wands. Whooping with glee, they then began waving the ribbons triumphantly in the air.

The fairies were taken completely by surprise, but they quickly raised their wands to cast a spell.

Unfortunately, they were too late. Jack Frost was already pointing his wand at them, and shouting a spell of his own. "Come, freezing wind and ice and snow. To the human world, Dance Fairies, GO!"

Instantly, an icy wind whistled through the throne room. Rachel and Kirsty watched in horror as the Dance Fairies were swept up in the freezing whirlwind and carried out of the window.

"So *that's* how we ended up in the human world!" Bethany sighed, as the images in the pool faded. "And that's how Jack Frost got our ribbons!"

Ribbons Whisked Away

"We *must* get the ribbons back," King Oberon declared.

"We'll all go to Jack Frost's ice castle immediately!" Queen Titania decided.

She waved her wand and Kirsty and Rachel heard a bell tinkling in the distance. A few moments later there was the sound of hooves, and a carriage made of shining crystal drew up outside the palace gates. The carriage was drawn by six unicorns with gleaming white coats and crystal horns. They came to a halt, tossing their snowy manes and neighing softly.

"Look, it's Bertram!" Rachel pointed out as the King and Queen led them over to the carriage.

Bertram, the frog footman, was sitting at the front of the carriage. He gave the girls a cheery wave.

Kirsty and Rachel climbed in and sat down next to thc King and Queen on pink velvet cushions. Meanwhile the Dance Fairies perched on the unicorns' backs, and the carriage set off through Fairyland.

It wasn't long before they'd left the beautiful green meadows behind. Rachel and Kirsty shivered as the temperature began to fall.

"There's Jack Frost's ice castle," Rachel said. The girls had visited the castle before, but it was still very scary-looking. It stood on a tall hill under a gloomy sky, and it was built of sheets of ice with towers topped by icy blue turrets.

"And there's Jack Frost!" Kirsty added, as a head poked out of one of the windows.

Jack Frost scowled when
he saw the carriage
approaching, and
ducked back inside
the castle again.

"Somehow, I don't
think he wants to
return the magic ribbons!"
Rachel remarked.

The carriage drew up beside the castle
and Bertram hopped down to help
everyone out. But, as they made their
way towards the heavy castle door, it
was suddenly flung open and Jack Frost
stalked out.

"You're too late!" he snapped. "The
ribbons are gone, and there's nothing
you can do about it!"

A great shriek above their heads made

37

Rachel, Kirsty and all the fairies glance upwards. They saw a goblin fly out of one of the castle windows, carried along by a huge whirlwind. He was clutching a pink ribbon which flapped in the breeze.

"That's my magic ribbon!" Bethany cried. She tried to fly towards the shrieking goblin, but the icy whirlwind pushed her back. In fact, the wind was so strong that Rachel, Kirsty and the others could hardly keep their feet on the ground.

"There's more of them!" Rachel shouted, pointing upwards.

Six more goblins were tumbling through the air. Each of them holding on to a different ribbon.

"I command you to return the magic ribbons, Jack Frost!" King Oberon cried. Battling against the wind, the King lifted his wand and murmured some magic words. Immediately, the wind dropped, but the goblins had already vanished. Rachel and Kirsty glanced at each other in dismay.

"You're coming with us, Jack Frost!" King Oberon said sternly. "And you'll stay under guard at our palace until all the ribbons are returned to the Dance Fairies."

"Oh, but you'll *never* get the ribbons back!" Jack Frost cackled. "I've told my goblin servants to hide in the human world, and there they'll stay! And besides..." he added, pausing and looking even more sly than usual. "Even if the fairies *do* find my goblins, they'll soon see that this time there's more to them than meets the eye!"

And he laughed even louder.

King Oberon sighed and waved his wand again. A swirl of fairy dust lifted Jack Frost off his feet and swept him into the royal carriage.

The doors slammed shut and Jack Frost's smile vanished.

"Girls, the goblins are hiding with the Dance Ribbons in the human world!" said Queen Titania, turning to Rachel and Kirsty. "Will you help the Dance Fairies to find them and get them back?

Rachel and Kirsty nodded solemnly.

"Each ribbon is attracted to its own type of dance," Bethany explained, "so each ribbon's magic will draw the goblin towards places where that ribbon's style of dance is taking place."

"Oh!" Rachel exclaimed. "We're going to the ballet tonight. Maybe the goblin with the Ballet Ribbon will be there!"

Bethany looked very excited. "I'll come with you, just in case!" she said.

Queen Titania was already lifting her wand to shower them with magic. "Good luck!" she called.

Looking more hopeful, the other
Dance Fairies waved farewell,
as Queen Titania's magic whisked
Bethany, Rachel and Kirsty away.
A moment later they were back on
the train.

"We'd better go and buy some
biscuits or Mum will wonder why we're
back empty-handed!"
Kirsty said, as
Bethany hid in
Rachel's pocket.

"We're almost
there, girls," Mrs
Tate said when Kirsty
and Rachel arrived back
from the buffet car. Mr Tate had
woken up and they were gathering
their things together.

Outside the station they took a cab
to the ballet. As they went inside
the theatre and took their
seats, Rachel and Kirsty
were amazed to see
how beautiful it was.
There were
sweeping gold
balconies, a domed
roof painted with
ballet scenes, and
golden chairs with
plush red cushions.

"Are you OK,
Bethany?" Rachel
whispered as the
lights began to dim.
Immediately the fairy peeped
out of Rachel's pocket and smiled.

The curtain rose, and Kirsty and
Rachel gasped as they gazed
at the wintry scene before
them. A huge frozen
lake surrounded by
leafless trees
covered most of
the stage, and
a full moon
hung in the
sky. Everything
was covered
with frost which
sparkled under
the bright stage
lights. Dancers in
feathery white tutus
were poised, motionless,
here and there.

"It's lovely!" Rachel breathed, and Kirsty nodded.

They waited breathlessly for the ballet to begin, but none of the dancers moved a muscle. Puzzled, Rachel and Kirsty glanced at each other as the spectators began murmuring in confusion.

"Why is nobody dancing?" whispered Mrs Tate.

"This is all very strange!" Mr Tate added.

"Something's not right," Bethany whispered to Rachel and Kirsty. "And I'm sure it has something to do with Jack Frost's goblins!"

Frozen!

Still the dancers didn't move. The curtain fell, and the mutterings of the audience grew louder.

"We must try to save the ballet!" Bethany said urgently.

Rachel nodded. "We need to find that goblin!" she said.

"Dad, can we go and get

a programme?" Kirsty asked quickly.

Mr Tate nodded. "Don't be long though," he said. "I'm sure the ballet will start again soon."

"We should start backstage," Bethany told the girls as they hurried out into the lobby.

"But we'll need to make sure that we're not seen," Kirsty pointed out anxiously.

They ran to the back of the theatre and cautiously Rachel pushed open the stage door. A doorman sat in a little booth just inside the entrance. "He's not moving," Kirsty whispered.

"And look!" Rachel added, as they went further backstage. "Neither is anyone else!"

All around them were stagehands who had been moving scenery, and dancers who had been warming up. But every single person was now completely frozen in place.

"They're as cold as ice!" Kirsty said, touching one of the dancer's arms. "Maybe Jack Frost has given his goblins a wand of ice magic."

"Listen!" said Bethany suddenly, "I can hear someone giggling!"

"It's coming from the other side of the stage," Rachel said.

Quickly the friends hurried across the curtained stage, weaving their way in and out of the motionless dancers. As they neared the other side, they saw a very strange sight.

A goblin wearing pink tights was struggling to get into a fluffy white tutu. He had jammed a pair of dainty white ballet shoes onto his feet, and around his head he had tied Bethany's pink Ballet Ribbon – larger now that it was in the human world – in a neat bow.

Rachel and Kirsty put their
hands over their
mouths to muffle
their giggles.

"I thought
the goblins
were supposed
to be hiding,"
Kirsty whispered. "This

one isn't doing a very good job of it!"

"The magic of the ribbons is so strong
that anyone who has one can't help but
dance!" Bethany explained, fluttering
out of Rachel's pocket. "Come on, let's
get my ribbon back!"

The goblin was so busy trying to
squeeze into the tutu, he didn't notice
Bethany and the girls until they were

right in front of him. Kirsty was glad to
see that he didn't seem to have a magic
wand, either.

"Give my magic ribbon back, please!"
Bethany said firmly.

The goblin scowled at her. "Go away,
pesky fairy!" he muttered. "I'm not
giving the ribbon back! I like being good
at dancing. And, even better, I'm ruining
the ballet for everyone else! Jack Frost is
going to be *very* pleased with me."

"That's mean," Kirsty said.

The goblin looked
thoughtful. Then
suddenly he
smiled sweetly at
Kirsty. "Well,
OK," he said.
"You can take

the ribbon, but you'll have to untie it for me. I did it up too tightly."

Rachel frowned, feeling suspicious. Why was the goblin being so nice all of a sudden?

"Kirsty, don't—" Rachel began. But she was too late. Kirsty had already stepped forward to undo the ribbon. And as she did so, the goblin touched her wrist and said, "Freeze!"

Instantly, poor Kirsty was frozen stiff.

Mooning Around

The goblin roared with laughter.

"Oh, no!" Rachel gasped, staring in horror at her frozen friend.

"Jack Frost must have given the goblins freezing powers," Bethany guessed. "So that's what he meant when he said there was more to the goblins than meets the eye!"

The goblin stepped forward, and reached out a big green hand towards Rachel. "Oh, no, you don't!" Bethany cried, waving her wand over Rachel, and transforming her instantly into a tiny fairy. Rachel zoomed away from the goblin's touch and joined Bethany, out of his reach.

"Teehee!" the goblin chuckled. "You can't touch me, or I'll freeze you too!" And still laughing, he ran onto the stage.

"What are we going to do about Kirsty?" Rachel asked anxiously as she and Bethany flew after him.

"Don't worry, Rachel," Bethany said,

as they perched in one of the cardboard trees. "The spell will wear off soon and Kirsty will be fine."

Below them on the stage the goblin had begun to dance. Rachel's eyes widened as he performed perfect jetés, pirouettes and arabesques.

"He's a brilliant dancer!" she said.

"It's only because he's got my magic ribbon," Bethany sniffed. "We must get it back!"

Rachel watched the goblin moving around the stage and in and out of the wings. He was touching all the ballerinas and stagehands as he went past them, and Rachel guessed he was making sure they all remained frozen.

Suddenly Rachel noticed the large, pale moon, made out of tissue paper, hanging from the top of the stage. It was suspended in the air from a rope, and as she looked at it, an idea popped into her head.

"Bethany," she whispered, "if the goblin was underneath the paper moon, we could drop it down on him and grab the ribbon!"

"Great idea, Rachel!" Bethany agreed eagerly. "It's very light, so it won't hurt him. But how will we get the goblin to stand underneath it?"

Rachel frowned. But before she could suggest anything, she saw Kirsty hurry onto the stage below. Kirsty was keeping a close eye on the dancing goblin, but she was also looking around for Rachel and Bethany. "The freezing spell's worn off and Kirsty's looking for us!" Rachel whispered to Bethany. "Maybe she can help us get the goblin underneath the moon."

Bethany nodded. "We'll have to be careful though," she whispered back. "We don't want the goblin to guess what we're up to!"

The little fairy waved her wand and a few magic sparkles drifted downwards, making Kirsty look up and spot her friends in the tree.

Rachel immediately pointed at the moon and then at the goblin, trying to explain to Kirsty that they needed him to be underneath the moon.

Rachel could see her friend frowning in concentration as she watched, but would she understand what Rachel wanted her to do?

Ballet Back on Track

For a moment Kirsty looked puzzled.
Then she nodded and turned away.
"I want that ribbon," she called to the
goblin. "And don't even *think* of trying
to freeze me again!"

The goblin scowled at her. "I can
freeze you any time I want!" he
snapped back.

"I don't think so!"
Kirsty said mockingly.

Rachel and Bethany
watched hopefully as
Kirsty casually moved closer
to the moon.

"I'll show you!" the goblin chuckled,
skipping gleefully towards her.

Just a few more steps! Rachel thought,
holding her breath. Kirsty moved away
a little and the goblin followed, his
hand outstretched to freeze her. Now
he was right underneath the
paper moon.
With a flick of her
wrist Bethany
sent a burst of
fairy sparkles towards
the rope which held the moon up.

66

The rope immediately untied itself
and the moon plummeted, knocking the
goblin to the floor.

"Agghh!" the goblin yelled in surprise.

Quick as a flash, Kirsty whipped the
magic ribbon from the goblin's head.
He sat up, looking furious but unhurt.

She tried to jump aside as the goblin grabbed at her wrist but she wasn't quick enough. Rachel's heart skipped a beat as the goblin shouted, "Freeze!" once more.

But, this time, nothing happened!

Kirsty looked relieved and waved up at her friends. "I'm fine!" she called. Bethany and Rachel flew down to join her.

"It looks like Jack Frost only gave you the freezing power while you had the ribbon," Bethany told the goblin with a grin.

Looking extremely sulky, the goblin

stuck his tongue out at her. "Well, we still have the other magic ribbons!" he snapped. "And I'll make sure we hang onto them!"

Scowling, he jumped up and ran off.

"Thank you so much, girls!" Bethany said joyfully. She sent a stream of magic fairy dust towards the ribbon in Kirsty's hand and it floated over to the little fairy, shrinking down to its usual Fairyland size as it did so. As the girls watched, the ribbon reattached itself to Bethany's wand in a cloud of pink sparkles, shining an even deeper pink colour as it did so.

"Now, hurry back to your seats while I put everything right here on stage," Bethany told Rachel and Kirsty. "Everyone will be unfreczing soon, and the performance will begin. Thankfully, now that I have my ribbon back, it should go perfectly!"

"Goodbye!" Rachel and Kirsty called to the fairy, hurrying towards the stage door. As they went, they saw the dancers and stagehands beginning to unfreeze.

"Let's get this show
on the road!" one
of the stagehands
declared.

Rachel and
Kirsty grinned at
each other. Then
they quickly bought
a programme and dashed
back to their seats.

"Just in time, girls!" whispered
Mr Tate as they sat
down. "The ballet's
starting now."
Rachel and
Kirsty gazed
eagerly at the
beautiful scene on
the stage once more.

The paper moon was back in its proper place again, and seated on top of it was Bethany. Rachel and Kirsty smiled as the little fairy waved at them before vanishing in a puff of silvery-white sparkles.

"This is going to be great!" Rachel sighed happily as the dancers began to pirouette across the frozen lake on stage. "But we can't forget that we've got six more magic ribbons to find."

"Yes, and we'll have to be careful of the goblins' new freezing powers," Kirsty whispered. "Still, I can't wait for our next fairy adventure!"

Now Kirsty and Rachel must help...

Jade the Disco Fairy

Read on for a sneak peek...

"Strike!" cheered Kirsty Tate, as Rachel's ball sent all ten pins flying at the end of the bowling lane.

"Hurrah!" Rachel cried in delight.

"That's your third strike of the game!" Kirsty's dad said, smiling. "Well done, Rachel."

"And it looks like you won the game, too!" Mrs Tate added, gazing up at the electronic scoreboard in front of her.

The girls went to see. Sure enough, flashing green letters spelled out 'RACHEL WINS' on the screen.

"Yay!" Rachel said. "I'm having

the best holiday ever – and it's only just begun!"

She and Kirsty grinned at each other. Rachel was staying with Kirsty's family for the autumn half-term holiday, and the two girls always had very exciting adventures whenever they were together. *Fairy* adventures! This time was no different. Only yesterday, they'd met the seven Dance Fairies, who'd asked for their help. The girls had said yes straightaway. They loved helping the fairies!

"Well, girls," Mr Tate said as the scoreboard flashed 'GAME OVER'. "It's time to take off your bowling shoes, and put on your dancing shoes. It's the school disco this evening, remember?"

"I can't wait," Kirsty said eagerly.

"Rachel and I love dancing, don't we?"

Rachel nodded, knowing Kirsty was thinking about the Dance Fairies. "Definitely," she replied. "Come on, let's go!"

Once they were back at the Tates' house, the girls got changed for the disco in Kirsty's bedroom. Rachel was wearing a pretty purple party dress, and Kirsty picked out a pink sparkly top and a pair of black trousers.

"I can't wait to see all your friends again," Rachel said, brushing her hair in front of the mirror.

Read Jade the Disco Fairy to find out what adventures are in store for Kirsty and Rachel!

Meet the Dance Fairies

Bethany the Ballet Fairy

the Disco Fairy

Rebecca the Rock 'n' Roll Fairy

Tasha the Tap Dance Fairy

Jessica the Jazz Fairy

Saskia the Salsa Fairy

Imogen the Ice Dance Fairy

Jack Frost has stolen the Dance Fairies' magic ribbons! Kirsty and Rachel must get them back, or dance everywhere will be ruined.

www.rainbowmagicbooks.co.uk

Meet the fairies, play games
and get sneak peeks at
the latest books!

www.rainbowmagicbooks.co.uk

There's fairy fun for everyone on
our wonderful website.
You'll find great activities, competitions, stories and
fairy profiles, and also a special newsletter.

Get 30% off all Rainbow Magic books at
www.rainbowmagicbooks.co.uk

Enter the code RAINBOW at the checkout.
Offer ends 31 December 2013.

Offer valid in United Kingdom and Republic of Ireland only.

Win Rainbow Magic Goodies!

There are lots of Rainbow Magic fairies, and we want to know which one is your favourite! Send us a picture of her and tell us in thirty words why she is your favourite and why you like Rainbow Magic books. Each month we will put the entries into a draw and select one winner to receive a Rainbow Magic Sparkly T-shirt and Goody Bag!

Send your entry on a postcard to Rainbow Magic Competition, Orchard Books, 338 Euston Road, London NW1 3BH.
Australian readers should email: childrens.books@hachette.com.au
New Zealand readers should write to Rainbow Magic Competition, 4 Whetu Place, Mairangi Bay, Auckland NZ.
Don't forget to include your name and address.
Only one entry per child.

Good luck!

The Rainbow Magic Reading Challenge

Well done, fairy friend – you have completed the book!
This book was worth 5 points.

See how far you have climbed on the **Reading Rainbow** on the Rainbow Magic website below.

The more books you read, the more points you will get, and the closer you will be to becoming a Fairy Princess!

How to get your Reading Rainbow
1. Cut out the coin below
2. Go to the Rainbow Magic website
3. Download and print out your poster
4. Add your coin and climb up the Reading Rainbow!

There's all this and lots more at
www.rainbowmagicbooks.co.uk

You'll find activities, competitions, stories, a special newsletter and complete profiles of all the Rainbow Magic fairies. Find a fairy with your name!